The whispers of the River

— BY THE SAME AUTHOR —

Already Published in French by BoD

- De l'Or dans votre jardin : Gagnez de l'argent avec   un élevage rentable (- Gold in your garden: Earn money with a profitable farm)

- La Promesse du Têt

The Whispers
of the River

© 2024 Gérard Ber
Édition : BoD • Books on Demand GmbH, In de Tarpen 42, 22848 Norderstedt (Allemagne)
Impression : Libri Plureos GmbH, Friedensallee 273, 22763 Hamburg (Allemagne)
ISBN : 978-2-3225-5451-5
Dépôt légal : Septembre 2024

To : Hélène, Jean-François, Mathilde et Alice

Foreword

This youth tale drew its inspiration from a trip
to Vietnam. The story and the names of the
characters are fictional.

The narrative takes place in 1962, in northern
Vietnam near the Mekong River, close to the
city of Can Tho...

Glossary of Vietnamese Terms Used:

- **Tết**: The Vietnamese celebration of the Lunar New Year, the most important holiday in Vietnam.
- **Ao Dai**: A long traditional tunic worn by Vietnamese women, often made of silk.
- **May Coong**: A hard wood from a tree in Vietnam, used to make tools and furniture.
- **Banh Chung**: A glutinous rice cake wrapped in dong leaves, eaten during Tết.
- **Nem Chua**: Spicy fermented pork rolls, often served as an appetizer or snack.
- **Bô Bun**: A Vietnamese dish consisting of rice vermicelli, vegetables, meat, and nuoc mam sauce.
- **Banian**: A sacred tree in Vietnam, often found in temples and spiritual places.
- **Dachshund**: A small dog breed with short legs, often referred to as a "teckel."

- **Biewer Yorkshire**: A breed of small dog with long hair, a variation of the Yorkshire Terrier.
- **Latanier**: A palm tree native to Asia, known for its large fan-shaped leaves.
- **Phu Quoc Pepper**: A renowned pepper cultivated on the island of Phu Quoc in Vietnam, appreciated for its unique flavor.
- **Ca Tru and Chèo Dances**: Ca Tru is a form of ritual music, while Chèo is a popular Vietnamese theater that integrates singing and dancing

Chapter 1: The silence of the Mékong

 At the edge of the great Mekong River, in a remote countryside, there was a small, peaceful village located in northern Vietnam, where a young girl named Peggy lived. She was pretty, slender, and full of energy, with large expressive eyes that shone with curiosity and emotion whenever she expressed her passions. Her long black hair fell to her hips.

She often walked barefoot to avoid wearing out the pair of blue sandals her mother had given her for her eighth birthday. Peggy loved feeling the warm earth under her feet, which gave her a sense of freedom and connection with the nature around her.

The war had not yet broken out when her father, then a newlywed, built a small house to house his new family.

Although the materials were made of wood, bamboo, and thatch, the dwelling always seemed solid. Out of love for his wife, he had made a table, three chairs, and a sideboard out of teak wood. Outside, on the earthen ground, he had placed four large cut stones and set a metal grate to support the cooking pot. This was where his wife, squatting, prepared the meals.

The house stood apart from a hamlet, near a vast rice field. Behind the small house was a well-tended garden where three banana trees, potatoes, tomato plants, peppers, and two rows of onions grew. The garden was protected by a two-meter-high bamboo hedge, shielding it from wild animals.

Peggy and her mother Leova lived peacefully in this rustic comfort. A a forty-year-old woman. She had a face that bore the marks of a life of work and sacrifices. Her features were gentle, but they were marked by the hard years of war she had endured with her husband.

Her sturdy hands were those of a worker always in motion, whether cooking, gardening, or maintaining the house. Leova's long hair had not turned gray but had become dull. She tied it in a simple bun, and for certain occasions, she braided it into two plaits that Peggy preferred.

The small circles around her *'eyes that shone like black olives'* were testimony to many sleepless nights that aged her by ten years. In the rice fields where she worked, she wore a large cone-shaped hat with a wide brim made of bamboo leaves, tied under her chin to protect herself from the sun.

There was a quiet strength and resilience in this woman that inspired respect and love from those who knew her. Despite having lived through many tragedies, her smile was always warm and welcoming. In her gaze was a deep affection that lit up her face when she looked at her daughter Peggy. She wore simple beige canvas pants and a white cotton shirt daily. This way of dressing suited both the traditional style and that of the rural woman.

On festive days, she wore an ordinary ***Ao Dai*** in green and yellow tones, the favorite colors of Vietnamese women and her late husband. During the war of independence, the **Can Tho** market was bombed. That day, Peggy, her only child, was injured. Her husband and many inhabitants perished in this tragedy. Fortunately, Peggy survived, but the explosion rendered the girl almost deaf.

To communicate with the child, her mother now used sign language. After her father's disappearance, the girl isolated herself in an inner world where only the presence of animals and nature made her happy. She found comfort in the silences imposed by her disability, turning this absence of speech into an inner strength that connected her even more to her environment.

Like her mother, Peggy wore a Chinese hat made of latanier leaves. Her black hair was often disheveled, a testament to her frequent explorations in the rice fields and pastures in search of quail eggs she brought home.

Despite her disability, she communicated with her hands with a liveliness that surpassed the need for words. Peggy used the sign language her mother had taught her and her facial expressions, often very animated, which resembled grimaces. Every morning before leaving for school, Peggy signed to her mother,

- I promise I won't linger on the way back. Leova, worried but confident, responded,

– Be careful and don't forget to say 'Good morning' to the teacher.

She watched her daughter walk away with a bit of concern. Her child brightened her dull and monotonous life; she loved her more than anything in the world.

To get to school, Peggy bravely walked three kilometers on dirt paths. Although she could not hear the birds' songs, she recognized the cuckoo, the barbet, the cormorant, the magpie, the tit, the kingfisher, and many other species. She only returned home around 4 PM. Sometimes, on the way, Peggy made a discovery she brought back.

– Look, mom, I found three quail eggs today!
– That's wonderful, my dear, I will cook them for your lunch tomorrow if you want.

Leova then prepared her daughter's only meal of the day: sticky rice with a rye bread cake, a tomato, and goat milk. Once a week, for her nutritional balance, she cooked fish or chicken. Isolated from her classmates due to her deafness, Peggy dreamed of having a friend, a companion with whom to share her long days. Her dearest wish was to care for a docile animal she imagined as the ideal companion in her solitude and games. But her mother did not want a dog.

– I wouldn't be able to feed it, she said.

So, Peggy secretly thought of a chicken.

She liked school very much. Like all her classmates, she greatly respected her teacher. Despite her deafness, Peggy was a gifted child. She had quickly learned to read and count. She loved her classmates, and affectionate bonds had formed with young Tao Thin, her close neighbor. Her parents had fled Cambodia after the war. This dramatic common point had sealed their friendship.

In the village where Peggy went every morning, a small building covered with a tin roof stood in the center of a large courtyard. Two windows and a large door surmounted by a faded sign composed the red brick facade. The rain had eroded the paint over many years, making the word '**SCHOOL**' barely legible. Inside, a single classroom hosted eighteen students.

The kind Madame Kea, the teacher, had authority over her children. She was a woman in her forties who had been teaching for ten years.

She came from **Can Tho** province and had been sent to the village two years earlier. She knew the sign language for the deaf. All the students adored her. She was always calm and smiling. The students were disciplined, so Madame Kea did not have to use authority over them.

Upon returning from school, Leova questioned Peggy.

- What did you learn at school today?
- We studied the planets in the sky. You know, mom, one day I want to travel far and discover the world.
- I'm sure you will, Peggy, you have an adventurous spirit.

After diligently finishing her schoolwork, Peggy helped her mother in the garden. They communicated in silence, their hands and gestures asking or posing a question without uttering a word.

– Look how well the tomatoes have grown! signed
  Peggy, with visible pride in her eyes.
– Yes, my dear. It's thanks to your care; you have the
  "Green Thumb," which means you are good at
  gardening. Her words gave Peggy confidence and
  made her forget her disability.

Before going to bed, the girl sat on the porch near the
entrance, where the setting sun still warmed the
gravel in the yard. Then, with precision, she drew
birds or imaginary animals in the dust with a piece of
reed. On school-free afternoons, Peggy loved to go to
the riverbank. Despite all the recommendations, her
mother was always anxious to know her daughter
was alone by the water.

  – Don't worry, mom, I will always be careful, she
    repeated to reassure her.

She quickly ate her meal, then, barefoot, dressed in
pants and a shirt, she took a narrow path that led her
in a few minutes to the refuge set up on the riverbank,
cluttered with reeds. She carried a small fishing net
made by her father, hoping to catch the shimmering
fish gliding beneath the water's surface.

This activity was not just a game but a way to feel connected to the wild nature and bring a bit of food to please her mother.

Hidden among the tall grasses, she skillfully cast and recast her nylon net, seeking to surprise the stationary fish under the dark water. The river was calm and seemed to be sleeping.

Peggy inhaled the slightly sweet and sour smell of the river and smiled. She loved the river. This scent reminded her of a dish her mother cooked on festive days with *Nuoc-Mam* sauce.

She dismissed this thought as she concentrated on her net plunging into the sparkling water. Suddenly, her face lit up at the sight of the fish caught in her net. A moment of pure magic in her daily life of silence!

Not far away, a large black **cormorant**, perched on the branch of a dead tree, its wings wide open, watched the fisher with its yellow eye. It coveted Peggy's fish, uttering hoarse "gra, gra" sounds while flapping its large black wings. Peggy was wary of the cormorant. She knew the bird's habits, capable of stealing her catch in a flash if left unattended.

So, after pulling the fish out of the net, she immediately put them in a small wicker basket to keep them from the predator's greed.

The afternoon was well advanced when Peggy took the path home, her fish basket full.

She walked briskly, her net under her arm, murmuring,

- Mom will be so happy; she will probably go to the floating market tomorrow to sell them.

Chapter 2: The Promise

Before dawn, as the first rays of the sun painted the horizon with a scarlet hue, Peggy was already awake, observing the garden from her bedroom window. The young girl felt a profound solitude, accentuated by the silence of an immobile space. She dreamt of her imaginary companion who would share her long days, filling the silence in which she was immersed with their presence.

This morning, she decided to speak (with her hands) once more about her wish to her mother. A wish often discussed but always refused. While preparing breakfast, Peggy gently tapped her mother's arm.

– Mum, for my birthday, I only want one thing: no toys, no books, just a chicken," she signed anxiously.

Her mother, hands busy mixing ingredients in an earthen bowl, set the spoon down with a resigned sigh. She was used to hearing her daughter's request. She looked at Peggy, and with both hands signed:

– My dear, you know what I think about your idea. Chickens are not meant to be friends. We raise them for our food. They are not pet in my house!

Peggy, with eyes full of fierce determination, was not discouraged. Clenching her fists against her chest, she continued naively.

– But Mum, she could be different. I will take good care of her, I promise you, she will not just be a chicken. I will consider her a friend.

Leova cast a gentle look at her daughter, the shadows of fatigue enhancing the tenderness of her expression. She knew how isolated her daughter felt, especially since her accident. After a moment of reflection, she took Peggy's hand. With a voice tinged with worry,

– And if this animal does not meet your expectations, if she does not become the friend you hope for, what will you do?

Peggy held her mother's arm, gently squeezing her fingers.

– Mum, I will be happy to take care of her even if things do not go as I hope.

Her voice became more insistent.

– Please, Mum.

Leova's feelings were mixed. She no longer listened to her daughter. A flood of images came back to her mind. She remembered the days of her childhood, walking the paths in this same village. At that time, she was Peggy's age. Her mother owned twelve laying hens that brought in a bit of money by selling eggs at the market.

One night, a fox entered the chicken coop, causing panic among the sleeping hens. The noise of the frightened chickens had drawn her husband, who chased the fox away. It was a terrible loss. Mina, her favorite laying hen, was among the victims of the fox.

This small tragedy had upset her. Two weeks later, her little sister Ley fell ill. The family did not have enough money. They had to buy medicine. Her mother had to resign herself to selling what was left of the hens to care for her daughter.

These painful memories were the reason for her refusal to Peggy. She had never told her this story. Leova feared her daughter would experience similar pain if her chicken was taken by a fox. Was Peggy's happiness worth taking this risk? Peggy gazed at her mother, her look filled with hope and sincerity, causing her mother's resolve to waver. Leova saw her daughter growing up, imprisoned in a world of silence, and her motherly heart wanted more than anything to bring her some joy.

- I agree, she said with a nod, for your birthday, I will go to the Can Tho market to buy your chicken. I have saved a bit of money from selling your last catch. But you must promise me to take care of this chicken !
- I promise, exclaimed Peggy with her hands, a broad smile lighting up her face as she jumped for joy.

Her mother's heart softened at seeing her child's excitement. Although this decision might complicate things, making her daughter happy was worth the risk.

– We will make this chicken your friend. I hope you find the companionship you seek so much with her.

Thus, with a light heart and full of hope, Peggy eagerly awaited the day she would meet her new companion, certain that she would bring a change to her imperfect world.

The next day, her friend Tao came to help. Together, they made a small chicken coop and a shed using some planks and bamboo, filled with straw where the chicken could sleep safely. Then, they finished the work with a wire fence to protect the chicken coop from foxes.

Now everything was ready to welcome the new resident.

Tao was born in Cambodia and was the same age as Peggy. Her mother was Cambodian, and her father, a

Frenchman with Norwegian origins, had participated in the technical study for the construction of the large hydroelectric dam in northeastern Cambodia. Like her friend, Tao had little known her father. Her mother liked to say that her daughter resembled her father.

It was easy to believe because Tao's eyes were light, almost blue, and her slightly curly Venetian blonde hair made the girls in her class jealous. Peggy's deafness and the disappearance of their father had solidified their friendship.

They were always together during recess but saw little of each other outside of school as Tao lived in a more distant village. Sometimes, Tao's mother would drive her to Peggy's house. Thus, the two girls spent an afternoon together. Peggy taught Tao the art of net fishing. She had learned that her neighbor had trained a cormorant for fishing.

> – How so for fishing? her friend had replied, surprised.

– Well, the fisherman ties a lace around the bird's neck, without strangling it, just to prevent it from swallowing the prey that gets stuck in its crop.

Peggy paused, then continued her story.

– The fisherman opens its beak to remove the fish from its crop.

– That's extraordinary! exclaimed Tao.

Peggy looked at Tao and wondered if her young friend had believed her story...

• **Chapter 3 : The Surprise**

Several weeks passed. Leova was preparing her trip by pirogue to the Can Tho market.

She remembered : Shortly after their marriage, she had asked her husband to build her a canoe. She no longer wanted to go to the Can Tho market by bus: it was too long and too tiring, she often repeated to him. The six-meter-long boat was built at the small shipyard in the city of Hué. The work of cutting and shaping an oak trunk imported from Laos took the workers two weeks. Then, the canoe was transported by river near the village. One year, the monsoon was very violent, the Mekong overflowed and carried away many boats. Like many villagers, Leova lost her canoe...

The sun rose on the horizon in a blazing flare, while the last stars faded in the morning sky. The mist, slowly pushed away by the first rays, gradually revealed the river. Peggy was still asleep when Leova left the house. She took the path leading to the river. She found her neighbor's pirogue moored near a pier. About four meters long, built with mangrove and teak wood planks, the pirogue was massive and seemed solid.

The boat's bow was decorated with brightly colored symbols and a traditional dragon design. The pirogue was narrow and shallow, making it easy to navigate the canals.

Leova carefully placed all the items she would trade at the market into the flat bottom of the boat: garden tomatoes, some aromatic herbs, and a bit of Thai rice. She untied the rope knot. Pushing the boat through the reeds from the bank, she let the river's current gently take the pirogue, which glided silently on the water. As she passed, cormorants and gray herons took flight. Only the regular splashing of the paddle in the water disturbed the silence. The boat passed houses on stilts that were still asleep.

As she approached, frightened ducks in their enclosures quacked loudly. After a few minutes of navigation, Leova saw the familiar silhouettes of the Can Tho floating market in the distance.

It looked as if many small, colorful houses floated above the waves. Pirogues had a mast with a bright

Chinese lantern tied at the top, swaying with the rocking motion. This was a distinctive sign: pirogues loaded with fruits and vegetables had a green lantern, those carrying fragrant flowers had a yellow lantern, and for poultry and fish, the lantern was red.

Boats came from all the Mekong canals. Some had gas engines, but most were maneuvered with a large paddle. Each vendor stood and shouted their offers to attract buyers' attention. The boats crossed and brushed against each other in a cheerful jumble that attracted curious onlookers and buyers from neighboring towns. Carefully, fruit-laden pirogues approached huge stationary boats crowded with tourists taking souvenir photos. Cameras clicked.

Skillfully navigating, Leova maneuvered her pirogue through this labyrinth of colorful boats. With a nod, she greeted the women pilots or exchanged polite words with those she recognized. Finally, Leova arrived at a pirogue with woven reed cages, from which chicken heads popped out, clucking. The humid, warm air was filled with cackling and a strong smell of droppings. Leova cautiously approached a pirogue.

– Chào buổi sáng (good morning), greeted the buyer, bowing her head. The two boats brushed against each other.

Leova scrutinized each cage, examining its contents, looking for a healthy occupant, preferably with white feathers. At the fourth cage, her eyes stopped on a chicken whose stillness contrasted with the other birds' agitation.

She asked the seller to show her and take it out of the cage. The seller presented the chicken, holding it firmly by the legs. Leova felt the softness of its feathers under her fingers. It was plump. That was a good sign!

The chicken's anxious eye and clucking convinced Leova that this was the right choice. She proposed exchanging the bird for some of her goods, then paid the difference with a hundred thousand dongs in crumpled bills.

Leova was satisfied. She carefully slipped the chicken into a jute bag. Peggy would be pleased, she thought. The atmosphere was heavy; a big storm was brewing, filling the sky with electric flashes. She needed to get home quickly.

After her mother left, Peggy had headed to school. When Leova docked at the pier, the threatening storm had moved west, sparing the small village.

Back home, Leova prepared lunch for her daughter.

At 4 p.m., the teacher whistled the end of class. The school quickly emptied of its students, and Peggy began the long walk home.

Near the front door, a surprise awaited her. A brown cardboard box, pierced with small holes, was placed on the stone step. Intrigued, the girl approached the object. The box was sealed with adhesive tape. The package was small. Could it contain anything other than what she hoped, Peggy wondered?

She hesitated to open it and instead pressed her eye against the holes. Clucking? Yes, she heard it. No doubt, she thought, there's a chicken in the box!

She slowly put the box down, and impatiently tore off the tape, lifting the lid. Inside, an adorable creature stared back at her. Its bright yellow eye followed every movement of the child. Its feathers were as white as snow, and a small pink comb stood straight on its head. The chicken had been confined for several hours; it only wanted to escape!

Peggy let out a cry of joy. Her wish had finally come true. She had convinced her mother. With both hands, she grabbed her new friend. She was happy.

- I will name her Picotte, she declared solemnly, with a radiant smile.

From the open kitchen window, Leova watched. In a firm tone, she taught the first rules.

- No chickens in the house. You must keep her safe in the garden in her shelter, and be careful with stray dogs and foxes. As for her food, she will have to manage!

Peggy quickly signed her visible impatience with her hands.

- Yes, Mum, I promise.

In her mind, she already had a plan to protect her young friend from all possible dangers.

The following days were filled with happiness. Peggy was delighted. Every morning before school, she visited Picotte, wishing her a good day, and every afternoon after school, she told her about her day. She gave her a bit of rice from her last meal. For Peggy, all these attentions became habits that made her proud and responsible.

One Sunday morning, as dawn struggled to brighten a sky streaked with gray clouds, Picotte let out loud cackling, punctuated with joyful clucks: "Cocorico, Cocorico!"

Fearing danger, a worried Peggy ran to the garden still in her pajamas. Arriving at the scene, she discovered her excited friend singing near a strange object.

Picotte had given her a gift! The chicken had laid her first egg. A beautiful, large white egg. An immense smile lit up her face as she rushed to surprise her mother.

She was out of breath when she saw her mother in the garden. Hiding her left hand behind her back, Peggy signed with her right hand.

–   Mum, guess what I have for you?

With a hint of hesitation, her mother replied.

–   An egg, my girl !
–   Oh Mum, I wanted to surprise you, how did you know?
–   When a chicken sings so loudly for a long time, it means she has laid an egg, and then you can go and find it in her nest.

This was a lesson Peggy would not soon forget.

• Chapter 4 : The Tết Celebration

Ben Do was the name of the village where Leova and Ley lived together. It was located five kilometers north of Can Tho near the Mekong River. The quickest way to reach the big city was by bus, but many villagers preferred navigating the river in a canoe on market days. Although the journey was longer, the boat allowed them to transport many items and foodstuffs. The riverbanks were lined with houses 'with feet in the water,' all built from bamboo and planks cut from *May Coong*, a hard and water-resistant wood.

Leova had never wanted her husband to build their house near the water. The Mekong could be unpredictable and overflow during the strong monsoon. Her little paradise, surrounded by rice fields, was bathed all year in an atmosphere of calm and greenery. That morning, the sky stretched infinitely, pure and crystalline blue. A brilliant sun kissed the countryside, while the warm monsoon breezes chased away the winter's humidity. In two days, the traditional Spring Festival would illuminate Ben Do, thought Leova, as the festive excitement would reach all the villagers.

The Tết ceremony was a very important moment for the villagers, especially for Leova, who regularly revered the spirits of the ancestors on this occasion. Her prayers testified to filial piety, intimately communicating with her deceased husband. She honored him with offerings of fruits and flowers, which she placed on the altar in plates. Candles were lit, and incense burned to honor the Buddha. With the Spring Festival, she knew a new year was coming, and with the new season, the fieldwork would begin.

To make a living, she had to work hard to produce her vegetables, selling them at the market twice a week. She also took care of a small rice field that provided her main food: rice. Her daughter would also have to help with cleaning and decorating the house. Meanwhile, the little girl ran through the countryside, picking colorful wildflowers like kumquats and peach branches, symbols of life and renewal. During the three days of Tết, the streets would be filled with music, vibrant with the rhythm of the celebration.

They would be adorned with colorful Chinese lanterns released at nightfall and large banners on which children had painted red and gold dragons that seemed to breathe fire. The sound of drums would resonate in the air, marking the steps of dancers twirling in the streets. This sound would be joined by the crackling explosions of firecrackers. The children's joyful cries would mix with the adults' laughter. Peggy would be deprived of this joyful music, but she would feel all its vibrations. For her and her family, these would be festive days marked by folk dances and culinary delights. Her friend Tao Thin would join the celebration. Together they would enjoy *Banh Chung*, a glutinous rice cake that her mother cooked wonderfully. Leova, animated by a secret hope, would go to the temple to honor the Venerated Goddesses of heaven, water, and mountains. She would pray that one day a new husband would bring joy to her heart and some money to her modest home.

This is what Leova was thinking. The rest of the story could have unfolded like this, but sometimes life holds surprises. For Leova, it was destiny knocking at her door...

On the eve of the first day of Tết, Peggy woke up earlier than usual. The sun slowly painted the horizon a pale pink. Excited by the preparations, she ran into the garden to check if Picotte was well, if she had found some grasshopper to peck, and wanted to tell her in her way about the special day ahead. The hen seemed particularly joyful, pecking enthusiastically at the few grains of wheat left around her enclosure. Peggy approached, promising her that after school, they would spend time together to announce her upcoming birthday, which coincided with the Spring Festival: her ninth birthday. The girl returned from school in the middle of the afternoon. The sun was high, and the heat enveloped the village in a gentle torpor. She immediately headed to the garden, eager to find her faithful friend. She opened the enclosure that protected the hen to give her fresh water. But, to her great astonishment, Picotte was not in her coop.

Her heart tightened with worry. She called softly several times for her friend.

— Picotte, Picotte...

No sign of the animal. The hen had disappeared, even though the gate was closed. Panicked, Peggy quickly went around the village, anxiously asking everyone she met if anyone had seen her hen. The neighbors shook their heads, mouthing words of consolation she didn't understand. Distressed and disheartened, she returned home, her mind tormented by dark thoughts about what could have happened to her friend. At the doorstep, she found her mother, who had just returned from the neighboring village where she had placed a bouquet of jasmine on her husband's grave. With her hands, she signed,

- Mom, Picotte is gone, she cried, her eyes overflowing with tears.
- Don't worry, my dear. She must have jumped over the enclosure and gone for a walk; she will come back, her mother reassured her.
- Come in. Aunt Ley arrived this morning from Saigon. She has prepared a feast for us and is eager to see you.

Ley was Leova's younger sister. Ten years younger, she had shown a rebellious temperament against the country's traditions early on. She couldn't stand living in the countryside where the smells and solitude bothered her and the work in the rice fields. Despite the distance, she remained devoted and grateful to her older sister, who had supported her after their father's death. Intelligent and ambitious, Ley had the chance to receive elementary education in Saigon, the big capital, thanks to the help of a distant uncle who had once wished to marry her. Later, with a secondary diploma, she easily found a job in Can Tho as a secretary at Hoà Phat and Masan, a large local company that manufactured agricultural equipment. Ley was younger and prettier than her older sister with a natural resemblance: the same black, fine hair that fell to her lower back, the same deep, dark, captivating eyes. Ley's were topped with carefully plucked eyebrows.

Thin lips formed a slightly oval mouth, with a small upturned nose. The whole harmonized and gave her face the expression of a beautiful, modern, dynamic young woman. Peggy's heart was heavy as she crossed the kitchen threshold.

She kissed her aunt, whose cheeks exuded an intoxicating fragrance of jasmine and banana, mingling sweetness and exoticism. Ley bought the perfume from the big city's bazaar, 'Miss Saigon.'

The sky-blue bottle represented a feminine silhouette. It was a cheap perfume that Peggy liked. The table set on an earthen floor was pleasantly arranged in the middle of the room. Several dishes were lined up on a tablecloth that Leova had decorated with wildflowers picked by Peggy.

The appetizing aromas of traditional dishes in preparation floated in the kitchen. Aunt Ley had brought specialties from Saigon for the occasion: dried seafood, **Nem chua**, **Bô Bun**, mung bean cakes, transforming the festive meal into a beautiful celebration of Vietnamese cuisine.

Despite the beauty of the table and the warmth of the family welcome, Peggy couldn't get the image of Picotte out of her mind. Sitting cautiously on a bench, she didn't try to hide her sorrow.

Her aunt and mother, laughing, exchanged confidences and memories, making wishes for the coming year.

Peggy was just starting to be distracted by the women's stories when a strange smell tickled her nostrils; a smell that did not come from the dishes already on the table. Intrigued, she asked timidly with a broad smile on her lips,

- What smells so good, Auntie ?
- It's a surprise, my Peggy.

Aunt Ley got up from the table and brought a large oval dish from the kitchen. Peggy's smile vanished instantly! Her eyes blurred at the sight of the dish her aunt had just placed before her. She realized it wasn't an ordinary recipe in front of her. It was a heavy and sustained smell that blossomed in her head and penetrated even into her heart.

It was a large chicken…it was… it was her faithful Picotte ! Her friend, lying there, well-roasted, on a bed of potatoes!

At that moment, Peggy's world collapsed around her. A muffled cry escaped her mouth, a mix of pain and a sense of betrayal. Her tear-filled eyes couldn't look away from the dreadful dish from which now emanated a sinister aroma!

Chapter 5: Consolation

The sudden and tragic end of Picotte plunged Peggy into terrible despair. Silence fell over the room like a shroud, and even the joyous cries from the village, carried by the wind, faded before the young girl's distress. Aunt Ley, suddenly realizing the extent of her mistake, paled, her trembling hands nearly dropping the dish she was holding.

– Peggy, I... I didn't know, she murmured,

the words lost in the heavy air of sadness. Leova, her eyes wide with shock and late comprehension, approached Peggy with open arms in a gesture of comfort that her daughter could not yet accept.

Peggy's tears flowed freely now, each sob a stark reminder of her loss. Unable to bear the sight of Picotte transformed into a mere festive dish any longer, she stood up abruptly. Overwhelmed by grief, her face hard, fists clenched, she left the room and ran towards the garden in search of refuge.

In the afternoon heat, the little girl nestled in the shade under the old *Banian* tree near the now-empty enclosure, where she had spent many hours watching and playing with Picotte. Leova and Aunt Ley exchanged worried glances before getting up to follow the young girl. They found Peggy curled up under the tree, her shoulders shaking with sobs.

Feeling powerless but determined to comfort her daughter, her mother sat down next to her, gently wrapping her arms around her shoulders.

– My dear little girl, we are both so sorry. Your Aunt Ley didn't know how much you cared for that hen. I was away for a moment while she was preparing the meal. She thought... we thought only about our tradition, not about your heart.

Touched by the sincerity and regret in her mother's voice, Peggy turned towards her, seeking comfort in her tear-filled eyes.

– Mom, why did she do this ?
– Your aunt didn't know about Picotte and you. She thought the hen was meant for the Têt meal.

– It was a dreadful mistake, but it's also tradition to eat poultry for the festival. She thought she was doing the right thing. She understands her mistake now. Your bond with Picotte was special. I should have warned her before I left. It's also my fault. Forgive me.

The initial shock of the revelation gave way to deep guilt and poignant regret. Leova blamed herself for not considering her daughter's feelings. Peggy took a moment to understand her mother's words, her grief gradually mixing with comprehension.
She knew these two women had not acted out of cruelty. They were respecting a tradition they deemed essential. Gradually, her mother's words and the warmth of her embrace brought some comfort.

Peggy felt her heart begin to calm. She tried to hold back her tears. The memories with Picotte were too fresh in her mind. She remembered running in the garden with her faithful hen, sharing moments of complicity. It was a poignant pain, as she realized the magnitude of her loss and the irreversibility of the situation.

– I'm learning, Mom. I know that sometimes,
  even the people we love can hurt us without
  meaning to.

These words she uttered showed great maturity for
her young age. Aunt Ley, who had been listening in
silence, added softly.

– And we learn that sometimes, we must think
  beyond our own experiences to truly
  understand those we love.

Usually so confident, Ley felt shaken by her niece's
distress. She deeply regretted her lack of foresight and
her ignorance of the deep bond between Peggy and
Picotte. Every word of comfort she spoke was full of
remorse. She had realized the importance of her
mistake and the terrible shock it had caused the young
girl she loved so much.

The following days were filled with reflection and
conversations as the family sought to heal together.
Despite its tragic beginning, the Têt festival became a
time of renewal not only for the months ahead but
also for family bonds. With the support of her mother
and aunt, Peggy had to learn to forgive,

understanding that love, even imperfect, remained powerful and strengthened family ties. Leova and Ley, witnesses to the child's pain, committed themselves to accompany her on the long path to healing.

Chapter 6:   Forgiveness

Peggy's heart was heavy with grief. Each beat resonated as a painful reminder of Picotte's loss. Yet, despite the pain, there was a spark of something new, something waiting to be explored and understood. It was hope, the kind that comes after tears, a gentle and silent hope that pushes through sadness like a young shoot through rich soil.

The Tết festival was now just a distant echo. The village had returned to its usual calm after the traces of the festivities had disappeared. That morning, as the small village slowly awakened, the sky lit up with an ochre color that the Master Sun had painted on the horizon and then placed on the rooftops. Peggy stood alone under the old banyan tree, the place where she had laughed and shared unforgettable moments with Picotte. The silence was deep, only disturbed by the murmur of the wind in the banyan leaves. Her mother joined her, carrying two small shovels and a young fig tree, a symbol of wisdom. The sapling was wrapped in a piece of burlap.

– Peggy, she began softly, I know nothing can replace Picotte, but I would like to plant this tree with you, for her, and to remind us that even after such a cruel trial, life continues and beauty can still bloom in our hearts.

Peggy looked at the sapling and then at her mother. Something in her gaze changed. There was acceptance in her eyes, a beginning of healing. The air was filled with the scent of honeysuckle flowers mingling with the smell of earth still damp with dew. In unison, they began to dig. Each shovel stroke was a small step towards reconciliation. Peggy felt the fresh soil under her fingers, a soothing sensation comparable to the warmth of the morning.

– Mom, I... I think I understand now, said Peggy, stopping to wipe the sweat from her forehead.
– The tradition, it was important to you, to all of us. But sometimes, it hurts. Maybe we should find a new way to celebrate it, a way that won't hurt us anymore.

Her mother nodded, a smile on her lips, touched by her daughter's wisdom and maturity.

– Yes, my dear. We can learn and we can change. That is also the message of Têt. It's not just about looking back, but also towards the future.

When the tree was planted, Peggy and her mother stood hand in hand, looking at their work. The tree was still young, its fragile branches swaying in the morning breeze, but in a few years, they would be strong and majestic.

– Thank you, Mom, for the tree, for helping me understand, for being here, murmured Peggy,

her voice filled with emotion. Her mother hugged her, a hug that said everything words could no longer express.

– I will always be here, Peggy, no matter what life brings us."

In the following days, Peggy gradually found her smile again. She resumed going to school. Her classmates had struggled to understand the depth of her pain, but they saw her transformation and greeted her with renewed kindness every day. After school, Peggy often stopped by the young tree. She would stand there, signing a few words to it as she had done for Picotte. It was her ritual, her way of remembering the lessons her mother had taught her about looking to the future. The Têt festival the following year arrived with its promises of good resolutions and joy.

Peggy and her mother, now closer than ever, prepared the festivities with a spirit of renewal. The tree planted in memory of Picotte had grown tall. It had become strong and vigorous, a constant reminder of the strength of love and the healing power of time. Peggy knew that the pain of losing Picotte would never completely disappear, but, like the tree, she would continue to grow, to blossom, and to find beauty in each new day.

The previous year's Têt had been overshadowed by a cruel tragedy. However, this year, a change was perceptible. The entire village seemed to vibrate with positive energy. The preparations for the new Têt festivities were progressing quickly. There was a palpable sense of joy and new promises in the air. Peggy could feel this energy. A certainty was growing in her, like an intuition. The Spring Festival would herald better days and bring happy news, marking a turning point in her life.

Chapitre 7 : The divine surprise

The monsoon had prolonged, pouring a great amount of water over the region. The Mekong had overflowed, flooding numerous small canals. This disaster had forced many families to flee far from their village. Luckily, Leova's house had not suffered severe damage, except for the thatch on the roof which had been blown away by the violent winds caused by the monsoon. Leova had asked her neighbor for help, who quickly replaced it.

The garden was now cluttered with debris of all kinds. They needed to clear all the rubbish quickly before the Têt preparations began. In Saigon, the bustling and polluted metropolis was also in a frenzy as the Spring Festival approached.

At 7 a.m., the air was still warm. An incessant parade of multicolored, sputtering motorbikes clogged the main street leading to the station. Ley had risen early to go to the Grand Central Terminal of the capital to take a train to Ho Chi Minh City. She had a special mission: to visit her old uncle Bảo, a big-hearted man and fervent defender of animals.

This humble, very old man was respected in his village. With his calm gaze, his dark eyes topped by thick eyebrows as white as his immaculate long beard, which almost covered his face. His head was bald, revealing a tranquil strength. He embodied a wisdom imbued with an almost royal nobility. In the past, the battle for the country's liberation had called upon his courage, and his wife liked to say that he had the demeanor of a national hero. Often sitting in a wicker chair, dressed in a white cotton *Ao Dai*, the old man would dream.

Ley had grown up far from her uncle Bảo. Had he forgotten her face? No, for he kept on his desk, in a golden frame, a photo of his young niece taken twelve years earlier. Bảo lived in a small apartment in downtown Ho Chi Minh City, with a balcony overlooking the grand Dong Khoi street, 900 meters long. It began at Commune-de-Paris Square and ended at the edge of the Saigon River. It crossed several squares and parks lined with luxurious buildings, old colonial structures, and modern offices.

Sitting in his chair, Bảo observed the constant hustle and bustle on this street below.

Ley knocked three times on the door.

— Hello, Uncle, it's me, Ley !

The old man, forewarned of his niece's visit, did not immediately recognize the young woman before him. He hesitated for a few seconds, then stepped aside to let her in.

— I am glad you came to see your old uncle before he disappears! he joked.

The last time Ley had set foot in Ho Chi Minh City was to celebrate her uncle's sixty-eighth birthday; he was now eighty.

— Tell me what brings you so far from Hanoi?

After a cup of green tea **'Shan Tuyết,'** Ley recounted in detail the tragic story of the hen Picotte, and how she wanted to surprise her young niece for Têt. Her plan was to bring her a young puppy. Uncle Bảo particularly loved dogs. He forbade the consumption of dog and cat meat in his neighborhood. This was still an ancestral tradition practiced in remote provinces of Vietnam. He fiercely campaigned for the government to ban this cruel custom by law. According to him, this practice tarnished the image of a modern Vietnam that the country's leaders sought to present to the civilized West.

The uncle listened to his niece without interruption.

> – I have just what you need,

he said, getting up to go to a backyard. A few moments later, he returned with a young dog in his arms, four weeks old. It was a little ball of fur with sparkling eyes and a tail wagging like a minnow out of water! The puppy was an adorable mix of **Dachshund** and **Biewer Yorkshire**. Its coat was dark with large white patches on its back and legs. Its big black eyes already showed great curiosity.

> – I am sure your niece will love him. This dog will make a good flock guardian and will scare away foxes.

Ley burst into hearty laughter.

– I named him GINGER, he added.

Ley took the animal in her arms, and it instantly rewarded her with a lick on the face.

– Peggy can find another name for him if she doesn't like this one," concluded Bảo.

The afternoon was drawing to a close when Ley left the building. A cool, dusty wind caressed her face, and she blinked. The street buzzed with noise and smelled of gasoline. The bus station wasn't far. As she walked, Ley felt a sense of pride. She had found the perfect gift, which now nestled in a box with holes. Ley took a bus to Can Tho, hoping to reach her sister's village before nightfall. She was eager to see Peggy's expression when she discovered her gift.

The bus was set to leave the city at 11 a.m. As she walked, Ley calculated the time it would take to reach Ben Tho. Can Tho was about 160 kilometers from Ho Chi Minh City. This journey would take at least three hours, not counting the numerous stops to pick up travelers who had been waiting on the route for a long time under the scorching sun and sometimes in the rain.

"The company demands profitability!" The bus wouldn't make any more stops once the maximum passenger limit was reached. Despite this, the driver would sometimes bend the rules to earn a bit more than the meager salary the company paid him each month. These deviations inevitably caused delays. Ley was aware of this and took these factors into account during her travels.

The vehicle was a Citroën. It had once belonged to the 'Autobus et tramways de Bordeaux' company. It dated back to the 1950s. It was an old banger! But it still ran! Ley took a seat in the middle of the compartment. The armchairs were covered with a greasy leather that must have once been red.
The seats of the vehicle had borne the weight of thousands of passengers, she mused. This spot had an advantage. The state of the roads and the kilometers covered by the Citroën had rendered its shock absorbers ineffective. They had suffered too much from the countless potholes that pitted the roads, where the asphalt had long since disappeared, making the old bus jolt.

If one sat at the front or the back, they had to hold tightly to the metal bar fixed above the bench to avoid constant bouncing and bumping. So, the clever young woman understood the trick and didn't hesitate to squeeze onto a bench of her choice when the bus was full to avoid standing.

Ley got off the vehicle at 3:40 p.m. under the scorching heat. The bus station was in the city center of Can Tho. She stopped for a moment to check on the puppy. Then, gently, she lifted the lid slightly. At the bottom of the box, curled up, the little puppy slept peacefully. Ley hesitated to pet him for fear of waking him. She resumed her walk.

To get to Ben Tho and her sister's house, she either had to take a taxi or walk the last five kilometers. She didn't hesitate long and headed quickly to the nearest taxi stand. A line of yellow cars was parked along the

curb. Ley approached the first taxi. "Take me to Ben Tho, please."

Chapter 8: Sparck

The yellow taxi dropped off its passengers a few minutes later. As it drove away, raising a cloud of dust, Ley looked at the narrow, rocky path ahead that would take her to her sister's house.

Despite the nearby flooded rice fields, by this late morning, the sun had managed to chase away the humidity. The scents of the Mekong, carried by a light spring breeze, tickled the young woman's nostrils.

It was a smell she loved, reminding her of her childhood in this family home, from which she had left very young to pursue her elementary studies. Just another hundred meters and she could finally rest.

At the beginning of her walk, Ley had thought it wiser to carry her burden on her head to relieve her arms. Although the puppy was light, it was starting to feel heavy.

Ley adjusted her position, determined to reach Leova's house quickly, where memories and reunions awaited. In the rice fields, women wearing large conical hats made of *latanier* were busy planting rice seedlings with their heads bowed. They formed colorful patches that contrasted with the green of the fields.

Leova was eagerly awaiting her younger sister. It was the first day of Têt. In the meantime, she had sent Peggy to the nearby neighbor to buy black **Phu Quoc** pepper to enhance her recipe. As the small house filled with the aromas of the dish in preparation and Leova was busy, Ley entered, shouting:

–   Hello, my darling older sister!

which startled her, causing her to drop her wooden spoon.

–   **Xin chao**, replied Leova, nodding her head in greeting.
–   Did you have a good trip ?

Ley responded with a broad smile.

–   A bit tiring, the state of the road is worsening, you know.

She placed the box on the floor.

–   Did you bring fruits and vegetables ?

inquired Leova, eyeing the box.

– No, but I brought a gift for Peggy.

But what would her sister think of this unexpected package?
Ley, curious but not questioning, approached the box, and to prolong the suspense, slowly lifted the lid.

– Let me introduce you to "**Ginger**!" exclaimed Ley.

Hands on her hips, Leova looked at the little creature with much astonishment, then burst into a nervous laugh.

– I suppose it's for Peggy ?

Leova thought: The dog would bring great joy to her daughter, but would she be fit enough to look after of a four-legged animal? While a hen doesn't require much attention, a dog needs daily food, water, and shelter at night. Ley sensed her sister's growing concern.

– A dog eats more than a hen; I only cook one meal a day for Peggy. How will I feed this animal ?

Her little sister anticipated this reaction.

– Is it really a good idea? Taking care of a puppy is a big responsibility for Peggy.

Ley quickly thought, searching for a convincing argument. She couldn't let her sister refuse the dog over this issue. Time was running out.

She feared Peggy's arrival before they reached an agreement. Suddenly, an idea struck her. Confident, she launched her argument.

- You could ask Quang the fisherman; he often has fish scraps he can't sell. Your friend Thao, the widow who took over her husband's butcher shop, could also save you some bits of fat.

Ley, assured of her argument, continued.

- Ginger is just a puppy; you'll only need to feed him once a day, so you'll have time to find another solution before he grows up.

She paused, took a deep breath, and then said,

- What do you think? It's a good idea, right ?

Ley fixed her sister with a slight, tense smile and placed a hand on her shoulder.

- You've convinced me, sis. The fish scraps and vegetables from our garden will be enough to feed him for now. I think Peggy should be back soon."

Indeed, the wait wasn't long. The little girl entered the room without noticing the box and its contents, which her aunt had cleverly placed under the small kitchen table. But how long before she discovered the surprise?

– Mom, here's the pepper you asked for.

For the little girl she was last year, for the image etched in her memory of the steaming dish on the table where Picotte was roasted, and although she had forgiven, Peggy still harbored some resentment towards Ley.

– Go and say hello to your aunt, ordered Leova, She brought you a gift for your birthday.

Peggy approached Ley timidly, who opened her arms to embrace her tenderly.

– Where is the gift you brought me ?

Ley stepped slightly away from the table to show her the box.

– Look at, it's under there !

Peggy pointed her finger,

– What's in the box ?

Without responding, Leova watched Peggy closely.

-   It's a gift for you, Peggy, to celebrate the new year and your birthday," Ley replied.

Peggy knelt down and lifted the box.

-   It's heavy! What's inside ?

The side of the box was pierced with several holes.

Peggy was a smart girl; she suspected that the box contained something alive, but she had no idea it was a little dog. She cautiously lifted the lid.

-   Wow ! exclaimed Peggy.

Her eyes widened at the sight of the puppy.

-   It's a dog, Mom! Oh, how cute !

Without any fear, Peggy plunged her hands into the box and grabbed the animal, which rewarded her with a lick on the face. Decidedly, it's a licking dog, thought Leova, witnessing the event and the wonder lighting up her daughter's face.

She smiled affectionately, convinced that Peggy was already attached to the creature, this little ball of fur, freshly freed from its box.

Peggy sat on the dirt floor with the puppy in her arms, visibly delighted. Ley knelt beside her,

– Ist's a girl. What name do you want to give her?

– "**SPARK**!" cried Peggy without hesitation.

– Yes, it's a perfect name for her.

– Then she added, I know nothing can replace your Picotte, but I'm sure this puppy will bring you a lot of joy.

With these comforting words, the family sat down for the meal. The Tết feast prepared by Ley, spiced with *Phu Quoc* pepper, glutinous rice, and dishes brought from Saigon, was a delight. It marked the beginning of a day full of emotions and surprises that would last late into the night.

After the delicious lunch, the four of them went to Ben Tho to admire the parade of yellow and gold dragons, animated by a lively, costumed troupe waving them with long sticks. The frenzied dances *Ca Tru* and *Chéo* accompanied by folk songs, resonated throughout the town center. The Tết festival ended as every year with a splendid fireworks display.

Once the festivities ended, life returned to its quiet and monotonous course. Ley went back home to Saigon. Peggy returned to her schoolmates. As she did with Picotte, after school, she visited the puppy to feed it, then after doing her homework, she spent all her time with her puppy. Together, they roamed the village streets and country paths. Their close relationship attracted the attention of Ben Tho's villagers. Everyone knew about Peggy's infirmity. They were impressed by how the dog seemed to intuitively understand Peggy's needs, anticipating her gestures and offering silent support.

Months passed. In this remote Vietnamese village, Peggy and Spark found their place in everyone's hearts. These two beings formed a powerful team, capable of bringing hope and support to their community, especially during difficult times. They embodied the strength of unconditional love and sincere friendship.

The two remained inseparables. Peggy had finally let go of Picotte and had reconciled with her aunt. The story of Peggy and Spark eventually spread beyond Ben Tho, inspiring families to believe in the strength of bonds that go beyond words, and to find strength in the silent company of a four-legged friend.

In this lost corner of the countryside where the culinary tradition was to sell dog meat for consumption, the bond and affection between Peggy and her puppy Spark sparked a change in behavior. Some villagers, witnessing this sincere and deep bond, realized that a dog could be a faithful and precious companion.

Under pressure from the local committee, the village chief had a decree adopted by the commune banning the sale and consumption of dog and cat meat. From now on, the teacher would teach kindness and respect for animal life.

Leova sent a message to her sister to inform her of this decision. Ley went to Ho Chi Minh City a few days later to meet her uncle again. She showed him the decree. Happy with this news, Bao published an article in the local newspaper, which did not create much reaction among the population. Nevertheless, the information eventually reached the state president's office, who promised to thoroughly examine the issue of animal protection. Uncle Bảo, the big-hearted man, concluded his article with Gandhi's words :

"The greatness of a nation and its moral progress can be judged by the way its animals are treated."

The End

Some Illustrations

«.. Peggy was slender and full of energy, with large, expressive eyes that sparkled with curiosity and emotion whenever she talked about her passions. Her long black hair cascaded down to her hips... »

" *...her face bore the marks of a life of hard work and sacrifices. Her features were gentle, but they were etched with the harsh years of war she had endured with her husband...* "

« ...To get to school, Peggy walked bravely for three kilometers along dirt paths. She liked school very much. Like all the students in her class, she had a great deal of respect for her teacher.... »

«… Peggy carried a small fishing net made by her father, hoping to catch the shimmering fish that glided beneath the water's surface. This activity was not just a game, but a way for her to feel connected with nature.… »

«... *Pushing the boat through the reeds from the shore, Leova let the river's current gently take hold of the canoe, which glided silently on the water. As she passed, cormorants and grey herons took flight. With impatient gestures...* »

«...With impatient gestures, Peggy tore off the tape and lifted the lid. Inside, an adorable creature stared back at her. Its bright yellow eye followed the child's every movement. Its feathers were as white as snow, and it had a small pink crest on its head.... »

« … Picotte had given her a gift! The hen had laid her first egg. A beautiful, large, white egg. … »

« … No hen in the house. You must keep her safe in the garden in her shelter, and be careful of dogs and foxes. As for food, she will have to fend for herself! … »

« … Ley's eyes were topped with carefully plucked eyebrows. Thin lips outlined a slightly oval mouth, and a small upturned nose gave her face the expression of a modern and dynamic young woman… »

« ...At that moment, Peggy's world collapsed around
her. A muffled cry escaped her mouth in a mix of pain
and betrayal! ... »

« …..Peggy left the room and ran towards the garden in search of refuge. In the afternoon heat, the little girl nestled under the old banyan tree near the enclosure…»

« … When the tree was planted, Peggy and her mother held hands, looking at their completed work. The tree was still very young, its fragile branches swaying in the breeze. … »

« … Often sitting in his wicker chair, dressed in a white cotton Ao Dai, Bảo embodied wisdom imbued with an almost royal nobility. … his wife liked to say that he had the demeanor of a national hero. … »

« … *The vehicle was a Citroën. It had once belonged to the 'Autobus et tramways de Bordeaux' company. It dated back to the 1950s. s…* »

« … *Peggy was already attached to the creature, this little ball of fur, freshly freed from its box…* »

The Tết Party